anythink

NO LONGER PROPERTY
OF ANYTHINK
RANGEVIEW LIBRARY
DISTRICT

D0382653

For my son, Arián, one of life's gifts.

For Joan Manuel Gisbert, Juan Farias, Joles Sennell, Gabriel Janer Manila and Gonzalo Moure,
friends of the word. — JS

To Carmen Correa Guimerá, an artist in Ropa Vieja, and many other things. — EU

JAVIER SOBRINO • EMILIO URBERUAGA

NIGHT SOUNDS

TRANSLATED BY ELISA AMADO

GROUNDWOOD BOOKS   HOUSE OF ANANSI PRESS   TORONTO   BERKELEY

In the rain forest

the sun hides behind the trees

And daytime sounds fade away,

As they do every day.

The moon comes up over the mountains

And night sounds whisper into being,

As they do every night.

The animals get ready to sleep.

The murmurs of the forest lull them And, little by little,

they fall asleep without even noticing.

If this goes on, all the animals in the rain forest will wake up.

WUAAAAA WUAAAA WUAA

Orangutan asks,

"Why are you crying, little one?"

"Because...hic...hic, because I'm cold."

"I'll get you a blanket.

Soon you'll be warm and then you'll stop crying

and everyone can go back to sleep."

AND SO THEY DO. BUT TEN MINUTES LATER... WHAT'S THAT NOISE?

WUAAA WUAAA

The forest animals wake up again

and some of them are cranky.

Tapir asks,

"Why are you crying, little one?"

"Because...huh...huh, because I'm thirsty."

"I'll get you some fresh water in a bowl.

You won't be thirsty anymore and then you'll stop crying

and everyone can go back

to sleep."

WUUAA WUUUA WUUU

THE FOREST ANIMALS WAKE UP AGAIN

AND SOME OF THEM ARE ANNOYED.

RHINOCEROS WALKS OVER AND ASKS,

"WHY ARE YOU CRYING, LITTLE ONE?"

"BECAUSE...snuff...snuff, BECAUSE I'M SCARED."

"I'LL BRING YOU A DOLL TO KEEP YOU COMPANY.

YOU WON'T BE SCARED ANYMORE AND THEN YOU'LL STOP CRYING

AND EVERYONE CAN GO

BACK TO SLEEP."

And so they do. But four minutes later... WHAT'S THAT NOISE?

WUAAAAH WUAAAAH WUAAAAH

It sounds like the roar of the waves.

Cuddled up inside an abandoned box, someone is sobbing.

Someone is crying louder and louder.

BUT... WHAT'S THAT NOISE?

WAAA WAAA WA

The forest animals wake up again

And some of them are irritated.

Bear comes close and asks,

"Why are you crying, little one?"

"Because...sniff...sniff, because I'm hungry."

"I'll get you some mango and honey candies.

You won't be hungry anymore and then you'll stop crying

And everyone can go

back to sleep."

AND SO THEY DO. BUT FIVE MINUTES LATER... WHAT'S THAT NOISE?

AND SO THEY DO. BUT THREE MINUTES LATER... WHAT'S THAT NOISE?

WUU WUU WUUUU

THE FOREST ANIMALS WAKE UP AGAIN

AND SOME OF THEM ARE ANGRY.

TIGER WALKS UP AND SAYS,

"WHY ARE YOU CRYING, LITTLE ONE?

"BECAUSE...snort...snort, BECAUSE I WANT MY MUMMY."

I'll go find your mummy. She'll cuddle you. You'll see.

A FEW MINUTES LATER, TIGER COMES BACK
SITTING ON THE MUMMY.

"Mummy!" cries the baby.

"Little one!" cries the mummy.

"Where were you?"

"I went to visit your grandparents, but now I'm back."

The little one jumps for joy and the ground shakes.

Elephant gives her baby a big kiss that

can be heard all over the forest.

"GOOD NIGHT, LITTLE ONE."

"NOW I CAN SLEEP," YAWNS THE BABY ELEPHANT.

FINALLY THE ANIMALS RELAX AND THEY ALL GO BACK TO SLEEP.

BUT ONE MINUTE LATER THE WHOLE FOREST CAN HEAR

WUU WUU WUUUUU

THE ANIMALS WAKE UP AND THEY ARE REALLY MAD.

THEY ALL LOOK AT THE LITTLE ONE, BUT IT IS NOT THE LITTLE ONE WHO IS CRYING.

It's a child in the nearby village.

Then the little one yells,

"A KISS. IT WANTS A KISS!
THAT CHILD MUST HAVE A KISS!
THEN WE CAN ALL GO BACK TO SLEEP."

And so they do.

The jungle murmurs lull them and all the animals
fall asleep and don't even notice that some of them are snoring.
Moments later... What's that noise?

TAP   TAP   TAP
    TAP   TAPPITY

It's raining. The rain comes back to the rain forest,
but the animals don't wake up.
They have been lulled
by the murmuring sounds
of the night.

First published in Spanish as Los Sonidos de la Noche
Copyright © 2012 by Ediciones Ekaré, Barcelona, Spain
English translation copyright © 2013 by Elisa Amado
Published in Canada and the USA in 2013 by Groundwood Books

All rights reserved. No part of this publication may be reproduced, stored
in a retrieval system or transmitted, in any form or by any means,
without the prior written consent of the publisher or a license from
The Canadian Copyright Licensing Agency (Access Copyright). For an
Access Copyright license, visit www.AccessCopyright.ca or call toll free
to 1-800-893-5777.

Groundwood Books / House of Anansi Press
110 Spadina Avenue, Suite 801, Toronto, Ontario M5V 2K4
or c/o Publishers Group West
1700 Fourth Street, Berkeley, CA 94710

We acknowledge for their financial support of our publishing program the
Canada Book Fund (CBF).

Library and Archives Canada Cataloguing in Publication
Sobrino, Javier
Night sounds / written by Javier Sobrino ; illustrated
by Emilio Urberuaga ; translated by Elisa Amado.
Translation of: Los sonidos de la noche.
ISBN 978-1-55498-332-2
I. Urberuaga, Emilio II. Amado, Elisa III. Title.
PZ7.S6825Ni 2013   j863'.7   C2012-905128-4

The illustrations were done in watercolor, ink and crayon.
Design by Irene Savino
Printed and bound in China

FSC
www.fsc.org
MIX
Paper from
responsible sources
FSC® C012521